THE STORM

Written by Jackie Goodyear
Illustrated by Leanne Fleming

Splish go the raindrops.

Listen to them spla*sh*.

Boom goes the thunder.

Listen to it **crash**.

Splish! Splash! **Boom! Crash!**

Listen to the storm.

I'm glad I'm inside,
where it's snug and warm.